The Glo Worm® Bedtime Book

by Lyn Calder

illustrated by Toni Scribner

Random House 🏠 New York

Library of Congress Cataloging-in-Publication Data: Calder, Lyn. The Glo Worm bedtime book. SUMMARY: Benjamin has trouble going to sleep until Glo Worm magically appears and tells him stories, poems, and songs about the inhabitants of Glo Land. 1. Children's literature, American. [1. Insects—Literary collections. 2. Literature—Collections] I. Scribner, Toni, ill. II. Title. PZ7.C1254G1 1986 [E] 85-61208 ISBN: 0-394-87804-3

Manufactured in the United States of America   1 2 3 4 5 6 7 8 9 0

Contents

Benjamin's Bedtime

"Benjamin, it's time for bed," called his father.

Benjamin was in the middle of building his best castle ever.

"I'm not tired," he called back.

Benjamin's father came into the room.

"That's a fine castle," he said. "But it will have to wait for you until tomorrow. Wash up and get ready for bed. Your mother and I will come to tuck you in."

Benjamin went to do as he had been told. While he was washing he made up a little song. Benjamin liked making up songs. He sang to himself:

"I made a big, fine castle,
I dreamed of a strong knight,
Who came to slay the dragons
And fight for what was right.
Then Dad came in and said to me,
'It's time for bed—Good night!' "

Benjamin laughed at his funny song. He wasn't feeling sleepy at all!

When he was through washing, Benjamin climbed into bed and called, "I'm ready!"

His mother and father came into his room. "You've been busy today," said his mother. "You must be very tired."

"Oh, no, I'm not," said Benjamin, sitting up.

"Well, just lie quietly," said his father, "and sleep will come."

They kissed Benjamin good night, wished him sweet dreams, then turned out the light.

Benjamin tried closing his eyes, but they seemed to pop open again all by themselves. Then he looked toward the window and saw a wonderful sight.

A set of glittering steps made out of stars reached into his room. Glo Worm came sliding down.

"Hello, Benjamin," said Glo Worm. "I hear you're having trouble sleeping."

"How did you know?" asked Benjamin.

"Your Glo Friends are always watching over you. I've come down to help," Glo Worm said.

"How can you do that?" asked Benjamin.

"In Glo Land there are lots of things to make you sleepy," explained Glo Worm. "Glo Grannybug always has a story to tell. And Glo Cricket knows lots of bedtime songs."

"I like stories and songs," said Benjamin.

"Then lie back, close your eyes, and listen," said Glo Worm.

So Benjamin settled down to listen with Glo Worm by his side.

The Night the Glo Drops Flickered
An Ancient Glo Land Legend

Once upon a time, long, long ago, two Glo Bugs were playing before bedtime. They were having a lovely tea party when along came a third Glo Bug looking for friends.

"May I join you?" he asked.

"No, you may not!" said one Glo Bug crossly. "Don't you see we're having a tea party?"

"And we only have two cups. One, two," said the second Glo Bug. "There is no teacup for you." And with that they went back to their tea party.

Seeing that the cups were only made of leaves, the lonely Glo Bug said softly, "I could make another cup for me." But the other Glo Bugs weren't listening.

When it was time to go to sleep, the two friends put away their tea set and got into bed. All at once the moon lost its smile and its Glo drops began to flicker. The two Glo Bugs rubbed their eyes in disbelief. When they opened them again, it was very dark.

"What's happening?" asked the first frightened Glo Bug.

"I don't know," whispered the second. "But listen. I hear somebody crying."

From a distant leaf came the muffled sound of a crying Glo Bug. Then the friends understood. Quickly they found the leaf.

"I'm sorry I was cross with you," said the first Glo Bug. "I was so busy with the tea party, I didn't stop to think about your feelings."

"I'm sorry, too," said the second Glo Bug. "Will you forgive us?"

The crying softened, and then it stopped. "I forgive you," said the third Glo Bug.

"We're having another tea party tomorrow. Will you join us?" asked the first.

The tearful Glo Bug brightened.

"I'd like that," he said.

Then the moon's Glo drops began to flicker and once again shine bright.

The Glo Bugs looked up. The moon was smiling and the Glo drops were shining just as they should be. Now the Glo Bugs knew that if ever a Glo Bug went to bed feeling sad, the moon's Glo drops would go out. The Glo Bugs decided right then to always be careful of one another's feelings.

Glo Bug's Bedtime Countdown
A Finger-Play Rhyme

(To begin, hold up all ten fingers. As each Glo Bug goes away, bend one finger down until both hands are closed.)

Ten little Glo Bugs
All in a line.
One went to brush his teeth,
Now there are nine.

Nine little Glo Bugs
Know it's getting late.
One went off to find her pillow,
Now there are eight.

Eight little Glo Bugs
Looking up toward heaven.
One left to count the stars,
Now there are seven.

Seven little Glo Bugs
Playing silly tricks.
One said he had enough,
Now there are six.

Six little Glo Bugs
Glad to be alive!
One started yawning,
Now there are five.

Five little Glo Bugs
Pick up toys from the floor.
One hums a lullaby,
Now there are four.

Four little Glo Bugs
Sleepy as can be.
One leaves, blowing kisses,
Now there are three.

Three little Glo Bugs
Sleepy through and through.
One puts on her nightgown,
Now there are two.

Two little Glo Bugs
See the day is done.
One sneaks away,
Now there is one.

One little Glo Bug
Beneath the moon's soft light
Makes a wish, then falls asleep;
Good night, Glo Bugs, good night.

The Missing Blanket
A Glo Land Mystery

Glo Spider was knitting the last row
of a baby-blue blanket when
she ran out of yarn.

"I'll just run inside and dye a
new batch," she said.

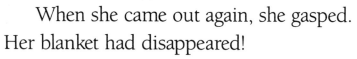

When she came out again, she gasped.
Her blanket had disappeared!

"I hope someone knows where it is,"
she thought. Then she headed off in
search of the missing blanket.

First she ran into Glo Grannybug down at Glo Pond, reading
a story to a small group of Glo Bugs. Glo Spider explained what
had happened.

"I'm afraid I haven't seen your blanket," said Glo Grannybug.
"I have been reading a very long story
and haven't taken my eyes from
this book for quite some time."

"Thank you, anyway," said
Glo Spider.

16

Next Glo Spider ran into Glo Snail and told him about her missing blanket. "Have you seen it?" she asked.

"No, I haven't," said Glo Snail, yawning. "I just woke up from a nice nap. You should try one."

"I can't now," said Glo Spider. "I must find my blanket."

A little farther on, Glo Spider saw Glo Bug, who was hard at work chasing shadows.

"I haven't seen your blanket," said Glo Bug. "But I do see a shadow behind you. So if you'll excuse me. . . ."

Glo Bug ran off to catch the shadow, and Glo Spider continued her search.

At Glo Meadow, Glo Cricket was practicing a new lullaby. She stopped to listen to Glo Spider's story.

"I was just going to try out this lullaby on a sleepy baby," she said. "Why don't you come with me? I'll help you look for your blanket when we get back."

She took Glo Cricket's hand, and together they raced down the Star Steps. When they reached a softly lit room, a smile spread across Glo Spider's face.

17

"Look!" she said. "I found my blanket!"

As Glo Cricket sang her lullaby, Glo Spider gently tucked the blanket up around the child's chin. Glo Spider was happy to have her blanket right where it belonged.

Shadows

A tiny leaf, a blade of grass,
So friendly in the day,
Become enormous, scary things
When shadows start to play.

Silently they come to life.
Watch them bend and sway,
Until brave Glo Bug comes along
To chase them all away.

Glo Lullaby

In a little cradle
Beneath the leafy trees,
Lies a sleepy baby
Rocking in the breeze.

Up above, Glo Butterfly
Waves her magic wand
And spreads her restful Glo dust
While she listens to this song.

20

Glo Spider spins a blanket,
She gently lays it down
While other special Glo Friends
Quietly gather 'round.

Hush, baby, hush.
Your Glo Friends will stay the night,
And they'll be there to waken you
With the morning light.

21

The Surprise Party

Glo Cricket was cleaning out her tree house when she heard a knock at the door. She looked out her window and saw Glo Snail.

"Hello, Glo Cricket," Glo Snail said. "Will you help me look for Glo pebbles down by Glo Pond?"

"I didn't know you had a Glo pebble collection," said Glo Cricket.

Glo Snail thought quickly. "I just decided to start one," he said.

It was Glo Snail's job to get Glo Cricket away from her tree house for a few hours. Glo Cricket didn't know it yet, but she was in for a big surprise!

As soon as they had gone, the others came out from their hiding places. "Won't Glo Cricket be surprised when she gets back!" said Glo Spider, who had started weaving Glo streamers for the party.

"Surprise parties are my favorite!" said Glo Butterfly as she hung Glo lanterns from the trees.

Glo Bug was blowing up balloons and Glo Snugbug was setting the table. Glo Snugbug counted out seven plates, seven napkins, seven forks, seven cups. "And now, seven bags of Glo treats and seven party hats!" he said happily.

Inside, Glo Grannybug was baking the Glo cake. "I hope they like my special new recipe," she said.

As Glo Butterfly was hanging the last lantern she saw Glo Snail and Glo Cricket in the distance.

"They're coming!" she called. "Everyone hide!"

When Glo Cricket saw the tree house, her face lit up.

"Surprise!" called her friends.

"Wow!" cried Glo Cricket. "I've always wanted a surprise party!"

"Let's get started then," said Glo Grannybug. "Who wants to play Blind Bug's Buff?"

Everyone wanted to play. Glo Cricket got to be "it" first, since it was her party.

Next they played Pin the Tail on the Glo Bug, and Glo Potato after that.

Then it was time for cake and treats. Glo Butterfly darkened the lanterns until the only light came from the moon. Glo Cricket sat at the head of the table and Glo Grannybug went inside to get the cake. When she came out, everyone sang,

"There comes a time just once a year
When Glo Friends gather from far and near,
They get things ready, and when all is right,
'Surprise!' they cry. 'Tonight's your night!'"

Glo Cricket closed her eyes, made her wish, and blew out every candle on her Glo cake.

As they were finishing their cake Glo Snail began to yawn. He covered his mouth to hide it, but it was no use. Everyone knew what would happen next. Glo Snail's yawns were very catching.

"Thank you for the party," said Glo Cricket sleepily. "I had a very good time."

"You'd better hurry now," said Glo Grannybug.

The Glo Friends scurried inside. Glo Grannybug tucked them in and kissed them good night.

"There's one more thing to do before we sleep," said Glo Butterfly. She knew she would have to work fast, since the yawning had already begun.

With not a moment to spare she waved her wand, spreading dream dust over her sleepy friends.

And just as they were drifting off to sleep, the stardust fell upon them, making sure their dreams were sweet.

Good Night, Benjamin

"I like surprise parties too," Benjamin said. Then, yawning a big, wide yawn, he added, "Glo Snail's yawns really *are* catching."

"Are you ready to go to sleep now?" asked Glo Worm.

"I think so," said Benjamin. "I'm feeling awfully tired. But first, may I sing you a song I just made up?"

"All right," said Glo Worm. "Then it will be time to sleep."

Benjamin began to sing:

"I look out my window and what do I see?
Star Steps reaching down to me.
I listen closely to hear Glo Cricket's song.
And isn't that Glo Grannybug humming along?
Glo Butterfly spreads her dream dust on me,
So I can sleep more peacefully.
Now I'll close my eyes with nothing to fear.
The night is safe when my Glo Friends are near."

When Benjamin finished he closed his eyes.
"Good night," said Glo Worm.
"Good night," Benjamin whispered, and dropped peacefully off to sleep.

29